WORLD HABITATS

Discovering
RAIN
FORESTS

Janey Levy

PowerKiDS
press
New York

Published in 2008 by The Rosen Publishing Group, Inc.
29 East 21st Street, New York, NY 10010

First Edition

Editors: Joanne Randolph and Geeta Sobha
Book Design: Julio Gil
Photo Researcher: Nicole Pristash

Photo Credits: Cover, p. 1 © Tim Laman/Getty Images; pp. 5, 6 (left, right), 7, 8, 10, 14, 17, 18, 21, 22, 24, 27, 28, 29 © www.shutterstock.com; pp. 11, 25 © Explosion 750,000; p. 13 © R.H. Productions/Getty Images.

Library of Congress Cataloging-in-Publication Data

Levy, Janey.
   Discovering rain forests / Janey Levy. — 1st ed.
       p. cm. — (World habitats)
   Includes bibliographical references and index.
   ISBN-13: 978-1-4042-3782-7 (library binding)
   ISBN-10: 1-4042-3782-8 (library binding)
   1. Rain forests—Juvenile literature. I. Title. II. Series.

   QH86.L486 2007
   577.34—dc22

                                                    2006036867

Manufactured in Malaysia

Contents

What Is a Rain Forest?   4

The Climate of Rain Forests   7

Where in the World Are Rain Forests?   9

Layers of the Rain Forest   12

Rain Forest Plants   16

Rain Forest Animals   20

The Importance of Rain Forests   24

The Amazon: The World's Largest
  Rain Forest   26

Protecting Rain Forests   28

Rain Forest Facts and Figures   30

Glossary   31

Index   32

Web Sites   32

What Is a Rain Forest?

When you think of a forest, what picture comes to your mind? Perhaps you imagine tall evergreen trees or deciduous trees, which have leaves that turn bright colors in the autumn then fall to the ground. Those are two forest types. A rain forest is another type. It has tall trees and, as you probably guess from the name, it gets a lot of rain. Most rain forests get more than 80 inches (203 cm) of rain each year. That is more than 6.5 feet (2 m) of rain!

A Very Old Biome

Rain forests have been on Earth for 70 to 100 million years. That means they existed when dinosaurs roamed the planet!

Tropical rain forests cover only about 6 or 7 percent of Earth's surface. However, they hold more than half of Earth's plant and animal species!

The warm, wet weather of rain forests creates the perfect conditions for the trees and plants that grow there.

The photo on the left shows a deciduous forest, and the photo on the right shows a pine forest.

That makes tropical rain forests one of Earth's most important biomes.

A biome is a community of plants and animals living together in a certain region. Climate does a lot to shape what kind of biome occurs in a region. Let's take a closer look at the climate of rain forests.

The Climate of Rain Forests

The climate is wetter in some tropical rain forests than in others. Some rain forests get only about 70 inches (178 cm) of rain each year. Others may get as much as 400 inches (1,016 cm). That is more than 33 feet (10 m) of rain!

Tropical rain forests are very warm throughout the year. The temperatures range from about 64° F (18° C) to about 95° F (35° C). There are about 12 hours of daylight every day.

The humidity, or dampness, in a rain forest can be about 80 percent all year.

7

This temperate rain forest is on the Olympic Peninsula, in Washington State. It is part of a larger rain forest that runs from Oregon to Alaska.

Temperate rain forests exist as well. Their climate is a little different. They get from 60 to 200 inches (152–508 cm) of rain every year. They have cooler temperatures than tropical rain forests. Temperatures rarely get above 80° F (27° C) in the summer. In the winter, temperatures may drop to around 35° F (2° C).

Where in the World Are Rain Forests?

The differences in climate between tropical and temperate rain forests result from their locations. Tropical rain forests occur within a very warm area known as the tropics, a broad band that runs around the middle of Earth. The tropics extend about 1,622 miles (2,610 km) north of the equator to a line known as the Tropic of Cancer. They extend the same distance south of the equator to a line known as the Tropic of Capricorn. Five continents have tropical rain forests. These continents are North America, South America, Africa, Asia, and Australia. About half of the world's tropical rain forests are found in South America. The Amazon, the world's largest rain forest, grows along South America's Amazon River.

Temperate rain forests occur farther away from the equator, where it is not as warm and the temperature changes more over the seasons.

The rains have washed minerals out of the soil of rain forests.

North America

Atlantic Ocean

Africa

Pacific Ocean

South America

This map shows areas around the world where there are tropical rain forests.

Temperate rain forests are usually found along coastal areas. They are found along the western coasts of North America and South America, along the coasts of some European countries, and along Australia's southern coast.

Layers of the Rain Forest

A tropical rain forest has four layers, each with special features. Trees in the top, or emergent, layer may be more than 200 feet (61 m) tall! They are widely spaced and project above the other trees. They receive lots of sunlight but must deal with very high temperatures and strong winds. Birds of prey, monkeys, bats, and butterflies live here.

Below this is the canopy, which also receives plenty of sunlight. Trees here are about 60 to 150 feet (18–46 m) tall. Their spreading branches form a roof over the layers below. Vines and epiphytes grow on the trees. Most animals live in this layer. They include insects, snakes, birds, and tree frogs.

Below the canopy is the understory. Little sunlight reaches here, so plants have adapted to living in dim light. Young trees, shrubs, ferns, vines, and mosses grow here. Tree frogs, jaguars, leopards, and insects live in this layer.

In tropical rain forests, like this one, most animals live in the canopy layer. In temperate rain forests, most animals live on the forest floor.

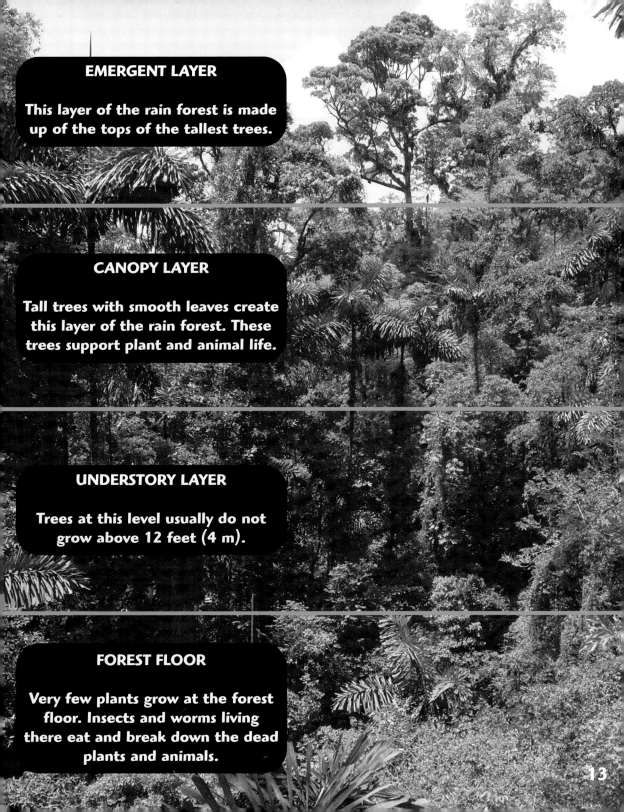

EMERGENT LAYER

This layer of the rain forest is made up of the tops of the tallest trees.

CANOPY LAYER

Tall trees with smooth leaves create this layer of the rain forest. These trees support plant and animal life.

UNDERSTORY LAYER

Trees at this level usually do not grow above 12 feet (4 m).

FOREST FLOOR

Very few plants grow at the forest floor. Insects and worms living there eat and break down the dead plants and animals.

The bottom layer is the dark forest floor. Less than 2 percent of the sunlight that falls on the canopy reaches this layer. As a result few plants grow here. Fallen fruit and dead leaves and animals cover the forest floor. Many insects and a few animals, such as wild pigs and giant anteaters, live here.

Temperate rain forests have three layers, the canopy, the understory, and the forest floor. The lower layers are home to many animals, including frogs, insects, birds, and many kinds of mammals.

What Big Leaves You Have!

Plants in the understory have large leaves to gather as much sunlight as possible. Some plants have leaves that turn to follow the Sun so they always get the greatest amount of sunlight.

These ferns grow in the understory of this eucalyptus rain forest in Australia.

Rain Forest Plants

Almost half of the world's plant species grow in tropical rain forests. Some tropical rain forests have 250 tree species in a 2.5-acre (1 ha) area. These include hardwood trees such as teak, mahogany, and rosewood. The wood from these trees is highly prized for making fine furniture and other expensive products. Rubber also comes from tropical rain forest trees. Other rain forest trees produce fruits.

Tropical rain forests yield over 3,000 kinds of fruit, including bananas, oranges, lemons, grapefruit, pineapples, figs, avocados, coconuts, and mangoes. Vegetables such as corn, potatoes, and squash grow there. Tropical rain forest plants produce coffee, Brazil nuts, cashew nuts, cocoa beans, cinnamon, vanilla, and black pepper. Imagine what your diet would be like without rain forest foods! Other tropical rain forest plants include ferns, mosses, palms,

Bromeliads are a family of plants that grow in rain forests. Many of these plants are grown by people all over the world for their beautiful flowers.

bamboo, epiphytes such as orchids and bromeliads, and more than 2,500 kinds of vines, or lianas.

Temperate rain forests do not have as many plant species, but some huge and ancient trees grow there. Western red cedars and yellow cedars can grow about 200 feet (61 m) tall and live about 2,000 years. Douglas fir trees can be almost 300 feet (91 m) tall. Alerce trees in Chile can live almost 4,000 years! Giant redwood trees in northern California are some of the world's tallest trees. In the summer of 2006, scientists discovered a redwood that is nearly 380 feet (116 m) tall. It is the world's tallest tree!

"Sticky Stuff" for Chewing Gum

Matter from the sapodilla tree, which grows in the tropical rain forest, has long been used to make chewing gum chewy. It is called "chicle," from a native word that means "sticky stuff."

The redwood forests of North America are temperate rain forests. The redwood trees can live as long as 2,000 years.

Rain Forest Animals

   About half of the world's animal species live in tropical rain forests. Different species are found on different continents. American tropical rain forests have more than 1,500 species of birds and 500 species of mammals. Insects form the largest group of rain forest animals, and American tropical rain forests have more than 2,000 species of butterflies alone. Birds include toucans and colorful parrots known as scarlet macaws. Mammals include bats, sloths, huge mouse relatives called capybaras, medium-sized wild cats called ocelots, and monkeys. One kind of monkey, called the howler monkey, uses its loud voice to warn enemies away from its territory. Fish, snakes, and brightly colored frogs also live in American tropical rain forests. Many of the frogs produce deadly poisons that native people apply to the tips of their arrows.

Mandrills live in the rain forests of western Africa. They live mostly on the forest floor.

The keel–billed toucan lives in the rain forests of South America. It is a poor flyer and mostly hops from tree to tree.

A 4-square-mile (10 sq km) piece of African rain forest could have up to 400 bird species, 150 species of butterflies, and 60 amphibian species. Some of the birds that live there are peacocks and the African grey parrot. African rain forests are also home to squirrels, monkeys, brightly colored baboon relatives called mandrills, wild hogs called bush pigs, gorillas, forest elephants, and chimpanzees.

Asian rain forests have elephants, mouse deer, orangutans, and tigers. They also have hundreds of amphibian and reptile species, including the king cobra. Thousands of bird and beetle species live there.

Rain forests in Australia and on nearby islands have animals unlike those anywhere else, such as tree kangaroos. They also have several kinds of parrots and many snake species.

Temperate rain forests have lots of insects, birds, and tree frogs. Mammals include bobcats, bears, raccoons, elk, deer, squirrels, and chipmunks.

Rain Forest Adaptations

Many animals in the rain forest are specially adapted for life in this biome. For example, toucans eat a lot of fruit. The toucan's long, large bill allows it to reach fruit on tree branches that are too small to support the bird's weight.

The Importance of Rain Forests

Rain forests are important in many ways to people everywhere. Everyone can enjoy the beauty of rain forest plants and animals. This beauty draws visitors from far away. The money they spend contributes to the region's economy. Rain forest woods and foods also have economic importance.

Many medicines come from rain forest plants. Since scientists have not yet tested 99 percent of rain forest plants, they expect to discover many more medicines.

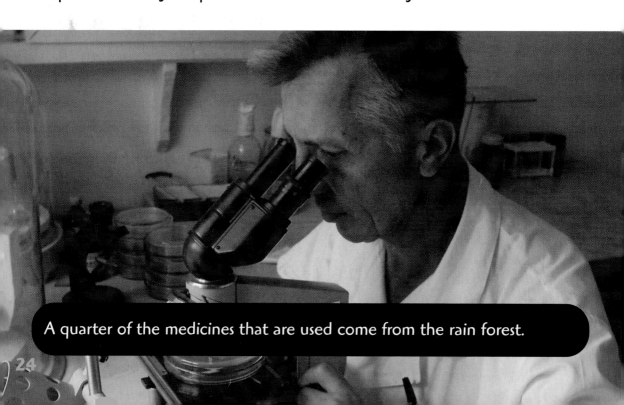

A quarter of the medicines that are used come from the rain forest.

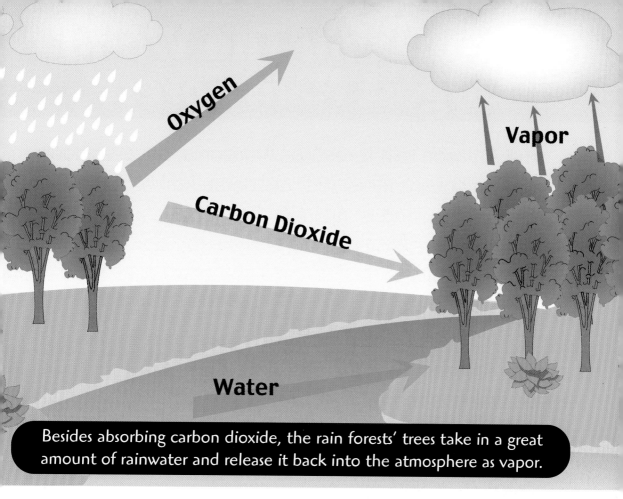

Besides absorbing carbon dioxide, the rain forests' trees take in a great amount of rainwater and release it back into the atmosphere as vapor.

Rain forests affect the world's climate. They help control temperatures by absorbing light and heat. The trees also take in huge amounts of carbon dioxide. Too much of this gas in Earth's atmosphere can cause temperatures to rise. Then they let out oxygen. All animals, including people, need oxygen to live. Life on Earth would be very different without rain forests.

The Amazon: The World's Largest Rain Forest

The Amazon rain forest, or Amazonia, covers about 2.4 million square miles (6.2 million sq km). About 60 percent of that land is in Brazil. Other parts are in Bolivia, Peru, Ecuador, Colombia, Venezuela, Guyana, Suriname, and French Guiana.

Amazonia's name comes from its mighty Amazon River, which is more than 4,000 miles (6,437 km) long. The river

Earth's Lungs

The Amazon rain forest has been called the lungs of our planet because it produces about 20 percent of the world's oxygen.

can be from 1 mile (1.6 km) wide to between 200 and 300 miles (322–483 km) wide where it empties into the Atlantic Ocean.

More than 2,000 fish species live in the river. More than 500 mammal species, 475 reptile species, and up to one-third of the world's bird species live in the rain forest. Scientists think about 30 million insect species live there!

The two-toed sloth lives in the rain forests of South America and Central America. This photo shows a mother and a baby.

Protecting Rain Forests

The world's rain forests are rapidly disappearing. Only about half of the area covered by rain forests in 1950 remains as rain forest. Some people believe 20,000 square miles (51,800 sq km) and 7,500 species vanish every year.

Many people are working hard to save rain forests. They work with governments to establish protected areas and educate people about rain forests' importance.

Logging and fires have destroyed much of the world's tropical rain forests.

The rain forest of Mount Waialeale, in Hawaii, receives one of the highest amounts of rainfall on Earth. About 450 inches (1,143 cm) of rain falls every year.

There are many things the rest of us can do to help. We can learn more about rain forest plants and animals, and the issues connected with rain forests and their disappearance. We can write letters to newspapers and the government suggesting ways to protect rain forests. We can reuse and recycle, rather than wasting Earth's resources. We can also do research to find out what products harm the rain forests, and then buy only those products that are not hurting our planet. We must all do our part to make sure the beautiful and important rain forest biome does not disappear.

Rain Forest Facts and Figures

- A tropical rain forest may have thunderstorms more than 200 days a year.

- A single tree in Peru may have more than 40 ant species.

- If tropical rain forests continue disappearing as fast as they are now, they could vanish in less than 50 years. The rain forests in Southeast Asia, the oldest rain forests on Earth, could be almost gone in just 10 years!

- About 80 percent of the U.S. and European diet originally came from tropical rain forests.

- A single rain forest park in Peru has more bird species than the entire United States has.

- A single pond in Brazil can have more fish species than all Europe's rivers have together.

- Only eight countries are larger than Amazonia.

- Every minute 28 billion gallons (106 billion l) of water flow from the Amazon River into the Atlantic Ocean.

- Scientists know less about Amazonia's canopy than they do about the bottom of the ocean.

Glossary

absorbing (ub-SORB-ing) Taking in and holding on to something.

bromeliads (bro-MEE-lee-adz) Plants in the pineapple family that store water at the base of their leaves.

carbon dioxide (KAR-bin dy-OK-syd) A gas that plants take in from the air and use to make food.

chimpanzees (chim-pan-ZEEZ) Animals that are related to gorillas but are smaller and spend much of their lives in trees.

deciduous (deh-SIH-joo-us) Having leaves that fall off every year.

epiphytes (EH-puh-fyts) Plants that get their food and water from air and rain. They grow on another plant but do not harm it.

equator (ih-KWAY-tur) The imaginary line around Earth that separates it into two parts, northern and southern.

mammals (MA-mulz) Warm-blooded animals that have a backbone and hair, breathe air, and feed milk to their young.

orangutans (uh-RANG-uh-tangz) Animals that are related to gorillas but are smaller and have red hair and very long arms.

sloths (SLOTHS) Slow-moving animals that live in trees and hang upside down.

species (SPEE-sheez) A single kind of living thing. All people are one species.

temperatures (TEM-pur-cherz) How hot or cold things are.

Index

A
Africa, 9
Amazon, 9, 26
Asia, 9
Australia, 9, 23

B
bats, 12, 20
biome(s), 6, 29
birds, 12, 15, 20,
   22–23
bromeliads, 19

C
carbon dioxide, 25
chimpanzees, 22
climate, 6–8, 25

D
deciduous trees, 4

E
epiphytes, 12, 19

F
ferns, 12, 16
fruit, 15–16

H
hardwood trees, 16

M
mammals, 15, 20,
   23
monkeys, 12, 20,
   22

N
North America, 9,
   11

S
seasons, 9
snakes, 12, 20
South America, 9,
   11
sunlight, 12, 15

T
temperature(s),
   7–9, 12, 25
tropics, 9

Web Sites

Due to the changing nature of Internet links, PowerKids Press has developed an online list of Web sites related to the subject of this book. This site is updated regularly. Please use this link to access the list: www.powerkidslinks.com/whab/rforest/